THE LEGEND OF THE
BUFFALO STONE

WRITTEN BY Dawn Sprung

ILLUSTRATED BY Charles Bullshields

VICTORIA · VANCOUVER · CALGARY

LONG AGO, in a place where rugged

mountain peaks stretched across the western skies, and snow
never seemed to melt from deep within their crevasses . . .

where, in the tall, reaching forests below, paths were worn by the
wily red fox and the white-tailed deer . . .

where excitement edged the cascading waters of the mountain
streams as fierce grizzly and black bears snatched up fish . . .

and where the curious snow hares and bold badgers dug holes
and dens into the walls of cliffs . . .

and where the grasslands were flatted out to prairie by thousands
upon thousands of grazing buffalo . . .

this was this place where lived Hanata.

Hanata had an adventurous spirit and loved to climb above the forests, up steep paths, to sit on rock ledges. Out beyond the cliff Hanata's heart and mind soared as the golden eagle soared, so effortlessly. She often watched the graceful bird dive suddenly for small, unsuspecting animals on the ground below. Hanata, too, searched for food—for the great buffalo, which her people called *innii*.

Hanata was a Blackfoot. The Blackfoot people moved their camps often to follow the migrating buffalo, which were always seeking new prairie grass. Hanata and her people travelled long distances on foot, for this was a time before horses. Their moccasins were black from walking through fields burnt by prairie fires. Dogs pulled travois, made with tipi poles and willow branches, that carried the people's belongings. Along the way, Hanata moved with the ease of a sure-footed mountain goat. She climbed the hills and rocky cliffs so that she could see great distances to search for the buffalo.

When they found the buffalo, the Blackfoot people built small rock piles shaped like the tipis they lived in. The men guided the *innii* down this pathway of stones that was longer than a mile. The women hid behind the cairns of rocks and leapt out suddenly to scare the bison.

The men then funnelled the buffalo down the narrowing trail to its end, where the animals were sent stampeding over a cliff. It was a difficult and dangerous task, for the great bison had sharp horns and hooves. With powerful legs and shoulders they ran swiftly. The sound of their pounding hooves was more deafening than a tremendous thunderstorm, and all felt the ground tremble.

At the base of the cliff, Hanata and the other women waited eagerly for the resounding clicking of the buffalos' hooves as the animals approached the precipice. They would soon go to work preparing the bison.

The *innii* provided for the Blackfoot. The bison meat was their food. Its hide, their clothing and tipi covers. Its bones, their tools and weapons. They were grateful to the Creator for this special gift.

Hanata used scraps of bison hide to make toys for the little children in her tribe. She made dolls using the skin and the hooves, and stuffed the dolls with animal hair. She used sticks and buffalo skin to make tiny tipis. With twigs she made little animals. The children were drawn to Hanata's peaceful spirit like a mountain bluebird to berries. At night they came to Hanata's tipi to help her build the miniature camp.

Before winter, or *sstoyii,* the Blackfoot prepared their food to last a long time. When the prairie grass and the leaves on the trees turned to blazing reds, fiery oranges, and sunny yellows, it was the sign that *sstoyii* was coming. The women cut buffalo meat into strips and dried them in the sun to make jerky.

Hanata made *mokimaani*. Using a stone tied to a willow handle, she dried and crushed berries, mint, and buffalo meat against a flat rock. She then combined this with pure buffalo fat.

Hanata always looked forward to berry picking. It meant time with her special friend, Koko, who was an elder. Hanata and Koko walked along the river watching the water tumble and swirl over rocks. They listened to the leaves whispering in the wind and the shrill cry of the hawk. They saw the deer grazing. Along the way, they picked each berry gently, careful not to break the living branches or leaves of the plant that provided the delicious fruit. Then they sat along the riverbank, and Hanata listened to Koko tell stories while Koko combed Hanata's long hair with a porcupine tail.

Like the bustling forest squirrels and chipmunks that stored great amounts of nuts and seeds in preparation for winter, the Blackfoot prepared and stocked large quantities of preserved food. They searched the surrounding forests for fallen trees to make and store firewood. With great respect for all that nature provided, the Blackfoot were most careful to take only what they needed. They moved their camps as the herds of buffalo moved.

The Blackfoot also searched for buffalo in the forests, where the animals sought shelter from the snow and severe winter storms. Hanata sometimes helped her father, Many Feathers, dress in wolf skins as he prepared to enter the woods with the other men. Draping themselves in wolf skins enabled the men to get closer to the bison and make their kill.

Almost every day Hanata would climb the hills and look out beyond the cliffs searching the prairies for signs of the *innii*. But after a fierce blizzard hit, the *innii* disappeared. Upon the cliffs Hanata watched, shivering, growing hungry and weary. Only a few elusive deer and elk had been hunted this season. The people were starving. Their food caches were empty. The sparse amounts of jerky and *mokimaani* had been divided amongst them all.

Hanata's spirit seemed to fall with the sun as it slipped behind the mountains. She remembered winter nights past, when the wise elders told their great stories of adventure while the children painted and played as they listened. Although her people were strong and did not complain, this winter Hanata knew many were weak with hunger and had grown ill.

Standing on a rock ledge, Hanata gazed solemnly down at her camp. She knew that some of her people were visited by the *Papai-tapiksi*, or Dream Beings, who came to them in their sleep and revealed designs from the dream world. These designs, which now adorned the tipis in Hanata's camp, were painted in honour of the animal spirits. The two black lines at the base of some tipis represented the buffalo trails they followed across the prairies. Circles depicted the puffballs that danced in the prairie grass. The pointed shapes were mountain peaks.

Hanata stared in wonder at the remarkable paintings of black buffalos, bears, and snakes, whose bold beauty could only be inspired by the spirits. Knowing that the painted tipis promised to bring good fortune and protect the families within, Hanata was suddenly filled with determination.

"We will not starve!" she exclaimed.

THAT FREEZING night Hanata camped on

the hillside wrapped in her buffalo blanket and stared into the fire. When at last she fell into a deep sleep, she dreamed that she was floating and wearing a beautiful elk-hide dress with exquisite quillwork! Wondrous clouds of indescribable colours swirled around her.

Then, out of this mist, a stone took shape. It sang to her. And then it spoke!

"I have come to you," the stone said, "because I have great pity for your starving people. You must travel to a cave at the base of the Mountain with Three Peaks. There you will find a rock resembling a sleeping bison. Take the rock back to your people—for it has great power and will bring back the buffalo."

Hanata thanked the stone and vowed to do as it said.

The stone whispered before it faded back into the mist, "Hanata, you were chosen to make this journey for you are humble and brave."

Hanata felt herself drop to the ground and awoke with a start.

In the morning Hanata told Koko about her vision. Koko helped her prepare for the journey, hopeful that Hanata had found a way to save the people.

Hanata felt the sharp snow bite the bottoms of her feet. Though the buffalo skin was wrapped high around her calves, the warm fur that once lined her moccasins had worn away. She was grateful for the fire she carried in a bison horn. As long as the sun stayed above the mountain peaks, Hanata needed to press on. She moved through the dense forest, staying on the trails made by animals of the woods.

Hanata slept little that night. From out of the blackness came the sounds of coyotes yelping, branches snapping, and the hooting of the great horned owl. She watched many shimmering stars dive from the sky towards Earth.

The next day, Hanata came upon a tree well and found fresh deer remains. Using a sharpened buffalo rib, she cut away any remaining meat and stored it in her parfleche.

When the sun shone at its highest point, Hanata at last saw the cave the stone had spoken of. She climbed up a ridge of rock to the dwelling and stopped short. On the ground leading into the cave were fresh tracks—the tracks of a huge mountain lion!

Hanata decided to use the doe carcass to lure the lion away from the cave. Trembling, she dragged the meat across the ground leaving a trail of blood and scent. Then she threw the meat over a cliff. Hanata's heart beat wildly like rain pelleting her tipi in a raging rainstorm. She hid behind a fallen tree and watched the mountain lion emerge from the cave.

With a deep, vicious growl the mountain lion followed the blood trail. When it was gone, Hanata dashed into the cave and frantically began to search. She heard the faint chirp of a bird and followed the sound. Then the firelight from her bison horn reflected off the stone, revealing its location. There it was, embedded in the cave wall.

Using her rib tool and a sharp rock, she dislodged the stone, which was indeed the shape of a sleeping buffalo, with four small bulges for legs. She took it outside and gasped at its brilliance. It was like holding a piece of a rainbow.

Just like in her dream, the stone spoke to Hanata. It taught her sacred songs and how to communicate with the *innii* to bring them back.

"But be warned!" it said. "My power will arrive with a fierce storm and it will appear as a lone bull. This buffalo must pass through your camp unharmed. If you allow this, the bison will come."

Back at the Blackfoot camp, Hanata's father gazed solemnly at
the top of his tipi, painted black as the night sky with unpainted discs
representing the Big Dipper and Pleiades. These stars were said to
be lost children who had gone to live in the sky. Many Feathers was
distraught thinking of his daughter alone in the cold mountains, where
wild animals were as hungry as his people.

The next day, Hanata sensed a quiet around her like that before
a storm. She felt the hairs on the back of her neck rise and a shiver
run down her spine. A growl from above broke the silence. Hanata
looked up terrified to see the massive mountain lion in a tree. It had
followed her—had stalked her!

It was about to pounce on Hanata like a coyote jumps on mice
in the prairie grass. Hanata backed away slowly, crouched down,
and grabbed a branch on the ground. Then she stood tall and held
it above her head. The cougar stared fearlessly, snarled viciously. It
lowered itself, ready to leap. Then Hanata felt the powerful magic of
the buffalo stone. She held out the stone, and the cougar cowered.
The huge cat leapt from the tree and scampered down the trail.

IN A DAZE, Hanata hurried towards home swift as a snow hare. She smiled, thinking about the return of her people's good fortune, the delicious buffalo stew they would prepare, the new skins for much-needed clothes, and the repairs to their tipis.

When Hanata arrived safely back at her camp, she told everyone about the power of the stone and the ceremony that would bring back the buffalo. The starving people were grateful. They were amazed at the stone's beauty and likeness to a sleeping buffalo.

That night the Blackfoot carried out the ceremony. They sang the buffalo calling songs. After dark, a harsh blizzard entered the camp. Trees fell. A swirl of snow moved strangely through the camp and—to everyone's astonishment—it was in the form of a lone buffalo. No one dared touch the animal!

By morning the storm
had passed, and a herd of
buffalo was grazing near the
camp! The people rejoiced!
The sacred buffalo stone
had saved them!

The Blackfoot people were indebted to Hanata and wished to honour her for her wisdom and bravery. The Buffalo Calling Stone, thereafter named the First Iniskim, would be kept in a sacred medicine bundle in Hanata's tipi. It would be used for spiritual ceremonies and when families needed help. Hanata's heart soared out of happiness for her people, who were strong and healthy again. It soared like the magnificent golden eagle!

Should you come upon an *iniskim*, may you see in it the form of a sleeping bison. May the sun rays bounce off the extraordinary gemstone, showing you colours you have never seen before, and, most importantly, may you feel the love and courage that Hanata felt when she took that difficult and dangerous journey to save her people.

Heritage House Publishing Company Ltd.
heritagehouse.ca

LIBRARY AND ARCHIVES CANADA CATALOGUING IN PUBLICATION

Sprung, Dawn, author
The legend of the buffalo stone / Dawn Sprung; illustrator: Charles Bullshields.

Issued in print and electronic formats.
ISBN 978-1-927527-41-2 (bound).—ISBN 978-1-927527-42-9 (epub).—
ISBN 978-1-927527-43-6 (pdf)

1. Siksika Indians—Folklore—Juvenile literature. I. Bullshields, Charles, illustrator II. Title.

E99.S54W45 2013   j398.2089ꞌ97352   C2013-903391-2   C2013-903392-0

Edited by Lara Kordic
Proofread by Leslie Kenny
Cover and book design by Jacqui Thomas
Cover images: *Grazing Buffalo* (front); *Return of the Buffalo* (back)

 This book was produced using FSC-certified, acid-free paper, processed chlorine free and printed with vegetable-based inks.

Heritage House acknowledges the financial support for its publishing program from the Government of Canada through the Canada Book Fund (CBF), Canada Council for the Arts, and the Province of British Columbia through the British Columbia Arts Council and the Book Publishing Tax Credit.

17 16 15 14 13   1 2 3 4 5

Printed in Canada